EMILY GRACE
and the
WHAT-IFS

A Story for Children About Nighttime Fears

by Lisa B. Gehring, MLIS

illustrated by
Regina Flath

Magination Press • Washington, DC • American Psychological Association

For Annabel, midwife extraordinaire. For Craig, Brett, Trey, and the Gehring Girls, our immeasurable joy. May your eyebrows always return. And especially for Kyle—ever supportive, forever loved…squirrel!—*LG*

For Violet, our most precious *what-if*, and for Dennis, whose love made this all possible—*RF*

Published by
MAGINATION PRESS®
An Educational Publishing Foundation Book
American Psychological Association
750 First Street NE
Washington, DC 20002

Magination Press is a registered trademark of the American Psychological Association.

For more information about our books, including a complete catalog, please write to us, call 1-800-374-2721, or visit our website at www.apa.org/pubs/magination.

Book design by Gwen Grafft

Printed by Phoenix Color Corporation, Hagerstown, MD

Library of Congress Cataloging-in-Publication Data

Names: Gehring, Lisa B. | Flath, Regina, illustrator.
Title: Emily Grace and the What-Ifs : a story for children about nighttime fears / by Lisa B. Gehring, MLIS ; illustrated by Regina Flath.
Description: Washington, DC : Magination Press, [2016] | "American Psychological Association." | Summary: Emily Grace runs into her room for bedtime, quickly drawing up her covers out of fear, soon wondering What if a big rhinoceros… or What if I wake up tomorrow a princess… or What if my eyebrows fall off… In the end, Emily wonders What if I close my eyes now and go to sleep?"— Provided by publisher.
Identifiers: LCCN 2015014372 | ISBN 9781433821066 (hardcover) | ISBN 1433821060 (hardcover)
Subjects: | CYAC: Bedtime—Fiction. | Fear of the dark—Fiction.
Classification: LCC PZ7.1.G44 E45 2016 | DDC [E]—dc23 LC record available at http://lccn.loc.gov/2015014372

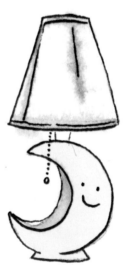

Manufactured in the United States of America
First printing November 2015
10 9 8 7 6 5 4 3 2 1

The night was dark
and it was time for
Emily Grace to go to sleep.

She ran through her bedroom door and jumped in her bed quickly so that nothing would get her.

She pulled the covers up to her chin, then smoothed them out
until there was not even one tiny wrinkle.

Then slowly, ever so carefully, she pulled her arms
under the covers so that all that was left peeking out
were her little nose and her big, brown eyes.

Emily Grace stared at
the ceiling with her
eyes wide open and waited.

It did not take long
for the what-ifs
to come out
from under her bed.

"What if a big rhinoceros charges out through my closet door and pulls all my covers off and I get cold and catch *pamonia?*"

"What if I wake up tomorrow
and I am a princess far, far away
from home, all by myself?"

"What if my eyebrows fall off
when I go to sleep
and they fly away forever?"

"What if I become a
pop star and make
a million trillion dollars
and then I lose it all?"

"**What if** a lizard comes out from under my bed and licks my face?"

Emily Grace noticed her stuffed bunny sitting quietly on the rocking chair in the corner.

She noticed the teapot on her pink table right where she had left it.

She noticed the white curtains fluttering in the gentle breeze from the slightly open window.

She noticed the
nightlight in the shape
of the moon, smiling
at her, as usual.

She noticed her strong,
tall tower and her
favorite teddy bear.

She noticed her pink tutu
and one ballet slipper
peeking out of her closet.

"What if I squiggle out my wiggles and then relax like my bunny under my covers?"

"What if I imagine I am in my favorite place, the beach, where I build oodles of sandcastles?"

"What if I tell my teddy bear,
tucked in so tightly, that I
will see him in the morning?"

"What if I breathe in slowly all the way up to the ceiling and breathe out all the way down to the floor? What if I close my eyes now and go to sleep?"

And that is exactly what Emily Grace did.

NOTE TO PARENTS AND CAREGIVERS
by Bonnie Zucker, PsyD

Bedtime is a trigger for many kids. Unlike the rest of the day, bedtime is a time in which children are expected to be alone. In addition, bedtime is often when children slow down and tune into themselves and reflect on their day; as a result, this may be when they express concerns and worries or exhibit separation anxiety. Fears about going to bed, worries that seem only to appear at bedtime, attempts to sleep with parents, and pleas for a parent to stay until they fall asleep are common.

Having a predictable routine and being available most nights at bedtime is necessary for your child's well-being; however, it is also important for children to learn how to self-soothe. The good news is that children can learn to cope with bedtime fears and fall asleep on their own. This book is a wonderful place to start.

HOW THIS BOOK CAN HELP
This story reflects an approach to coping with nighttime fears that applies the principles of acceptance and commitment therapy (ACT). The main goal of ACT is to prevent "experiential avoidance," which occurs when someone deliberately avoids an unpleasant feeling. Instead, the individual learns to be mindful and to tolerate discomfort, "sitting with it" until it dissolves or lessens in intensity to a manageable level. The individual discovers that he or she can handle feeling uncomfortable and can get used to the situation once he or she stays in it long enough (a process called "habituation").

This book illustrates what happens when, instead of avoiding her fears, Emily Grace faces them. She stays with them without reacting to them, changes her thoughts about them, and ultimately is able to cope with her fears and go to sleep on her own.

HELPING YOUR CHILD
COPE WITH NIGHTTIME FEARS
Bedtime struggles often result in lost sleep for children and their parents. Sleep deprivation has profound effects on attention, memory, school performance, mood, and even how glucose is absorbed in the body. Luckily, there are ways to teach your child to self-soothe and go to bed on his or her own. The following are some suggestions for helping children learn these important strategies.

Validate your child's feelings. Your child will benefit from knowing that you truly understand her fears. Try saying something like, "I know this is hard for you," or "I'm sorry it feels so scary at night." Comments like these will help to mirror, or reflect, your child's feelings, which will help her feel understood. Then you can explain that the goal is for her to learn how to cope with her fears and not let her fears influence her or the family's behavior. Say, "In our family, the kids need to be able to go to bed on their own," and that this is something all kids can learn. Emphasize that fears at bedtime are common, and she needs to learn how to cope with them.

Try relaxation strategies. After reading the story to your child, point out how well Emily Grace was able to soothe herself: she relaxed like her stuffed bunny, imagined a peaceful scene in which she felt good, reassuringly tucked her teddy in, and took a long, calm breath. The following are some similar relaxation strategies that you could try.

Progressive Muscle Relaxation: Tensing and releasing each muscle group in the body is one form of relaxation. Going through each part of the body, starting with the hands, and moving to the arms, shoulders, back, stomach, legs, feet, and face, have your child tighten and hold, then release and relax each muscle group one at a time, until eventually your child's whole body is relaxed. Ask your child to notice how his muscles feel when they are tense and how they feel when they are relaxed. This promotes more awareness of muscle tension in the body.

Imagery: Ask your child, "What kind of relaxing scene can you imagine?" If your child doesn't readily come up with a relaxing scene, you can offer one, such as being at the beach, lying in a hammock, or resting under a tree in a forest. Ask your child to use all five senses to imagine being there. The goal is to create the same relaxed thoughts and feelings that one would experience if one were actually there.

Calm Breathing: Practice lower diaphragmatic breathing: have your child breathe in through his nose and out through his mouth, very slowly, allowing the air to slowly travel down all the way to his lower belly, below his belly button, while his chest remains still.

You can also teach one-nostril breathing by breathing in and out through only one nostril while keeping the mouth and other nostril closed, again very slowly in and very slowly out.

Use distraction. In addition to learning relaxation techniques, children can use distraction to take their mind off of their fears. For example, you may read to your child or do puzzles with her. You can ask your child to make lists—for example, of fruits and vegetables, or girls' names and boys' names. Once your child has practiced with you, she can use these techniques on her own.

Teach your child positive self-talk. Your child can also try using coping self-talk to reduce his anxiety. Teach your child to send himself positive messages such as, "I am scared but I can do this," "What would someone who is not scared right now do?" and "I must face my fears." This allows your child to develop an internal sense of control in a scary situation, and promotes a sense of confidence that he can handle it! Before bed, remind your child to use these skills and tell him that if he feels scared, he can practice being brave. Reassure your child that he can do it—just like Emily Grace!

Practice alone time. It is also recommended that your child practice being in her room alone during the day, and that she can be comfortable playing alone. This can be practiced gradually, starting with ten minutes and moving up to 30-40 minutes.

Consider sleep training. The research on "sleep training"—which aims to get your child to fall asleep in his own bed, on his own without a parent present—indicates that it not only leads to better quality sleep but also makes your child a better sleeper (falling asleep easily, sleeping longer) in the long run. In addition, sleep training does not harm the child nor does it interfere with attachment. And if that's not enough, research has found positive effects on maternal mental health!

When sleep training, you need to gradually remove yourself from your child's room, allowing him to learn how to fall to sleep on his own. If he is sleeping with you in your bed, a good first step is to get him back in his bed and his room, even if you need to sleep with him there for a temporary period. Explain that he is going to start sleeping on his own and falling asleep by himself. Be confident and say, "I know you can do it."

Once you start the training, he will likely come out of bed and try to go into your room. Each time, you should direct him back to his room. After putting him to bed during your typical bedtime routine (e.g., story, lullaby, brief cuddle), the first time

he comes out of his room, you can walk him back and quickly tuck him back in. The second time is different: you don't go with him but you stand in the doorway of your room until he returns to his room and tucks himself back in. Ask him to call out to you once he is back in bed to let you know he did it. If he refuses to do this, in a calm, firm voice explain that he has a choice: he can either go back and tuck himself in by himself or you will go in your room and close and lock the door. The third time is a bit more challenging, as you won't open your door but instead will say something like, "You can do this. I know it's hard but you can face your fears. I love you." You can make two or three comments like this before you stop responding, and your child will eventually go to bed by himself (albeit after crying or screaming).

In the beginning, your child can put up quite a fight to not make this change; this is normal and expected. Being 100% consistent is key; if you open the door sometimes, it teaches your child that if he screams and cries, you will eventually come out. Rather, you need to teach him that you are predictably going to stay in your room, and that he needs to fall asleep by himself. By doing this, you are also endorsing his ability to do it himself. While it usually takes four to five challenging nights before he goes to bed seamlessly, once he learns it, the bedtime process will become a breeze. It requires a lot of strength on your part, but you are creating the conditions for your child to fall asleep on his own, and for you to be able to have a better bedtime yourself. This will be a gift for your child and whole family.

Finally, if your child continues to experience difficulty at bedtime, including excessive worries that interfere with falling asleep, it may be useful to meet with a psychologist or therapist to provide additional help to you and your child.

Bonnie Zucker, PsyD, *is a clinical psychologist specializing in the treatment of childhood anxiety. She is the author of* Anxiety-Free Kids *and* Take Control of OCD, *and co-author of* Resilience Builder Program *and two relaxation CDs.*

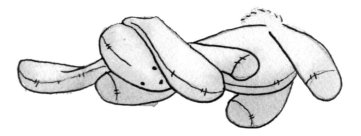

ABOUT THE AUTHOR

Lisa B. Gehring, MLIS, earned her master's degree from Louisiana State University's School of Library and Information Science. She has been a teacher and principal at a school for children with learning differences, and believes in empowering children to face and work through their fears. She loves to find the funny in life, convinced that laughter is one of life's greatest gifts. She lives in south Louisiana (Geaux Tigers!) with her husband and "granddog." Lisa uses Emily Grace's skills and many more to manage her own "what-ifs."

ABOUT THE ILLUSTRATOR

Regina Flath is a graphic designer and illustrator with a passion for books: reading them, designing them, and illustrating them. She graduated from the University of the Arts in 2009 with a BFA in illustration. She is the cover designer and cover illustrator for the David A. Adler series "Danny's Doodles." *Emily Grace and the What-Ifs* is her picture book illustration debut. When she's not making books, she's usually making something else, like herbal medicine, homemade lotion, socks, handspun yarns, or dinner. When Regina needs to relax before bed she likes to drink a cup of herbal tea and think of quiet forests. She lives with her husband Dennis, daughter Violet, and two crazy cats. Visit Regina at reginaflath.com and hear about her upcoming adventures by following her on Twitter @reginaflath.

ABOUT MAGINATION PRESS

Magination Press is an imprint of the American Psychological Association, the largest scientific and professional organization representing psychologists in the United States and the largest association of psychologists worldwide.